For Max – B. K. W.

For R. McS., R. D. I. – M. S.

First U.S. edition 1993
Text copyright © 1993 by Barbara Ker Wilson
Illustrations copyright © 1993 by Meilo So

Bradbury Press
Macmillan Publishing Company
866 Third Avenue
New York, NY 10022

Macmillan Publishing Company is part of the Maxwell
Communication Group of Companies.

First published in Great Britain in 1993 by Frances Lincoln, Ltd.
Apollo Works, 5 Charlton Kings Road, London NW5 25B.
Printed and bound in Hong Kong
10 9 8 7 6 5 4 3 2 1

LIBRARY OF CONGRESS CATALOGING-IN-PUBLICATION DATA
Wilson, Barbara Ker, date.
    Wishbones / by Barbara Ker Wilson ; illustrated by Meilo So. —
1st U.S. ed.
        p.   cm.
    Summary: In this Chinese version of the Cinderella tale, Yeh Hsien
uses magic fishbones to dress herself in finery for the Cave Festival,
where she loses a slipper in fleeing from her wicked stepmother.
    ISBN 0-02-793125-0
    [1. Fairy tales. 2. Folklore—China.] I. So, Meilo, ill. II. Title.
PZ8.W682Wi   1993
398.21—dc20
[E]   92-26993

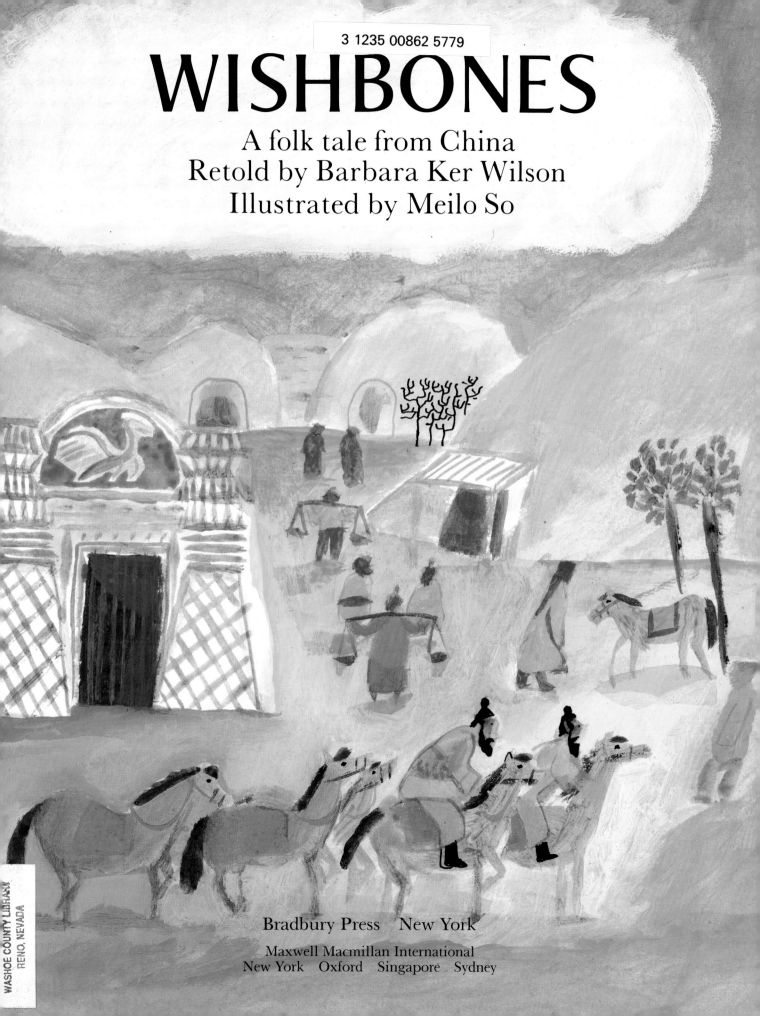

WISHBONES

A folk tale from China
Retold by Barbara Ker Wilson
Illustrated by Meilo So

Bradbury Press   New York

Maxwell Macmillan International
New York   Oxford   Singapore   Sydney

Thousands of years ago, in a cave among the hills of China south of the clouds, there lived a chieftain called Wu. Wu's first wife had died, leaving a daughter, Yeh Hsien.
Her father loved her dearly.

But Wu's second wife, who had a daughter of her own,
was unkind to her stepdaughter. Every day, she forced Yeh
Hsien to chop wood and sent her to draw water from deep
wells in dangerous places.

One day, while drawing water from a mountain pool,
Yeh Hsien saw a small fish with red fins and golden eyes.
Such a fish had never been seen before.

   Yeh Hsien caught the fish, brought it home to the cave,
and put it in a bowl of water. She fed it on grains of rice
saved from her own plate.

Each day, the fish grew larger and larger. At last, it was too big for the bowl, and Yeh Hsien moved it into the pond that lay close-by the cave.

Whenever she went to the pond, the huge fish would rise to the surface and pillow its head on the bank. But it would appear only for Yeh Hsien, never for anyone else.

"I should like to talk to that fish!" Yeh Hsien's stepmother said to her own daughter one day. "I have often waited by the pond, but it will not appear for me."

Then the stepmother thought of a cunning trick. That night, when Yeh Hsien came home tired from her hard day's work, her stepmother said, "Poor Yeh Hsien! How shabby you look in your worn-out coat. Take it off. Let me lend you my beautiful new jacket."

Yeh Hsien was astonished, but she did as she was told and put on the jacket. It felt warm and comfortable after her threadbare old coat.

The next day, Yeh Hsien was sent off on a long journey into the hills to gather herbs. As soon as she was out of sight, her stepmother put on Yeh Hsien's old coat and hid a sharp knife up her sleeve. "Now we will see about that precious red-and-golden fish," she told her daughter.

She went to the pond and called to the fish. The fish,
believing it was Yeh Hsien standing there, leapt from
the water and laid its head on the bank. Immediately,
the cunning stepmother killed it with her sharp knife. Then
she took it back to the cave and cooked it for their supper.

"This is the best fish I have ever tasted," Wu said, smacking his lips. His wife smiled. She did not tell her husband that it was Yeh Hsien's fish. After supper, she buried the fishbones in the dunghill outside the cave.

Imagine Yeh Hsien's sorrow when she returned to discover her fish had gone! She went to the pond and called, but in vain.

As she stood weeping, an old man with unkempt hair and a ragged coat appeared as if from the sky and stood before her.

"Don't cry, Yeh Hsien. Your stepmother killed the fish and buried its bones in the dunghill. But those bones are magic. Hide them, and whatever you wish for will be granted."

Yeh Hsien did as she was told, and she found, just as the old man had said, that she could have anything she wanted by wishing on the fishbones. Before long, she had jewels, finely carved jade, and embroidered silk robes hidden away in her corner of the cave.

Soon, it was Cave Festival time, when the people of the hills south of the clouds gathered to celebrate and make music. Yeh Hsien's father and her stepmother and stepsister set out to join the feasting, but Yeh Hsien was left to guard the fruit orchard behind the caves. Her father was sorry to leave her, but he did not dare say anything, for fear of his wife.

Yeh Hsien longed to go to the Cave Festival. No sooner was her family out of sight than she took off her everyday clothes and dressed herself in a shining blue-and-purple robe, with violet silken slippers upon her small feet. All these the magic fishbones had brought her. Then she set out for the festival.

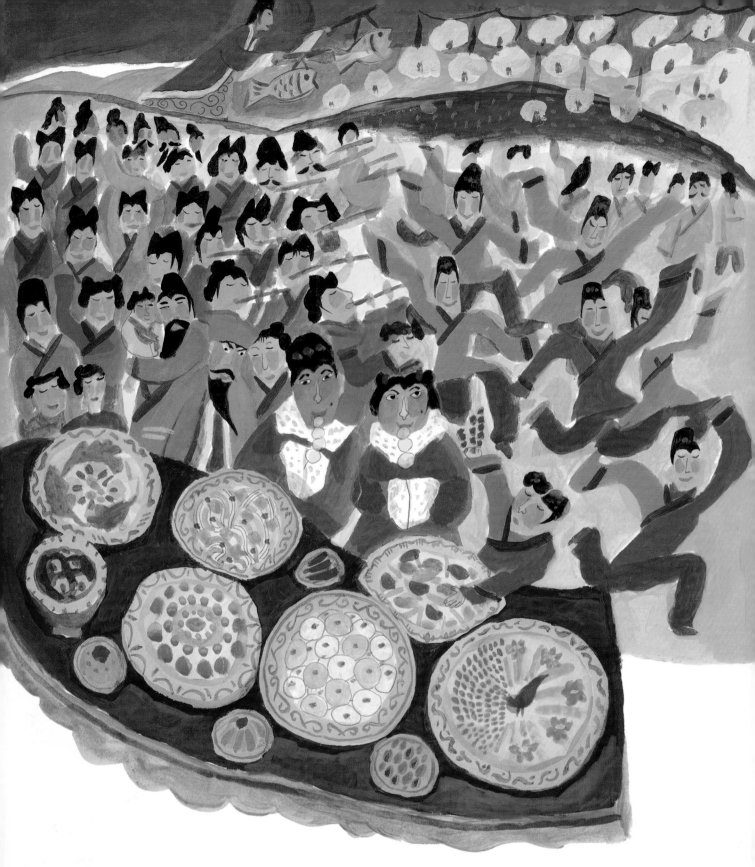

How Yeh Hsien enjoyed herself! She ate sweet bean cakes, laughed, and listened to the music, tapping her feet in their new violet slippers. She was dazzled by the lights of a hundred lanterns.

Later, as her eyes became used to the lights, she glanced about and saw her stepmother and stepsister looking at her in a puzzled way. Perhaps they recognized her!

Seeing their frowns, Yeh Hsien grew frightened. She ran away, and as she fled a silken slipper fell from her foot.

When her stepmother came home, she found Yeh Hsien asleep beneath a mulberry tree, wearing her everyday clothes once more. "How could I have imagined that the beautiful woman in the blue-and-purple robe at the festival was my wretched stepdaughter?" she asked herself.

Now, not far from that place lay the Kingdom of T'o Huan. After the festival, the cavepeople found Yeh Hsien's violet slipper and took it to the King of T'o Huan, who at once bought the precious object.

The young king commanded all the women of his household
to try on the slipper, but it proved too small for even the
tiniest foot.

"I will find the lady to whom this slipper belongs!"
the king declared. "She shall be my queen!"
He sent out messengers with the precious slipper
to search the countryside.

At last, they came to Wu's cave. First, Yeh Hsien's
stepmother tried on the slipper; it was far too small for her.
Next, her daughter thrust it on her foot, but it was too small
for her, too. Last of all, Yeh Hsien tried the slipper. It fitted
her tiny foot perfectly.

While her stepmother and stepsister watched in astonishment, Yeh Hsien ran to her corner of the cave and put on the matching violet slipper and her fine blue-and-purple robe. Then the messengers took her back to the young King of T'o Huan, who made her his wife and queen of all the land.

And what happened to those magic fishbones, Yeh Hsien's wonderful wishbones? She took them with her to T'o Huan, but the king wished for so much jade and jewelry and silk and gold during the first year of their marriage, that at last the fishbones refused to grant any more of his desires.

"Husband, you have worn out their magic," Yeh Hsien gently chided him.

The king was deeply ashamed. He buried the fishbones near the seashore, and later the tide washed them away. They have never been found to this day.